Sea Cl

Human Advance book 1

Contents

Chapter1 Getting Started

Chapter 2 Your Environment

Chapter 3 Local Measurers

Chapter 4 Building the Organisation

Chapter 5 Coping with the Backlash

Chapter 6 National Measurers

Chapter 7 Multinational Measurers and Coping with the Backlash

Chapter 8 Consolidation and the Future

Chapter1 Getting Started

Bryan Prentice was dissatisfied with his lot. He was sixty seven years old, retired, not well off but by no means poor. His worry was that the older he got the less control he seemed to have over his life which appeared to be slipping inexorably into a grey mediocrity. He had resigned himself to not ever making an indelible mark on the world back when he passed his fiftieth birthday and now found himself consumed with an impotent rage against a world intent on repeating the mistakes of the past over and over again.

Each day he went for a walk into the local centre for a coffee and to pass an hour or so reading in the coffee shop, making no contact with the people who flowed around him as he sat in isolation. Today the book he had been reading had descended into pointless drivel and not for the first time he was convinced he could have made more of what at first had seemed a promising idea. As a consequence he was taking a different and longer route home to fill some of the time between his return and the evening meal.

As he tramped along, eyes downcast occasionally wiping spots of fine drizzle from the lenses of his spectacles his mind drifted aimlessly. Wet weather was one of his pet hates. Ever since his hair had receded to the point where he had more face than was desirable he found cold rain a particular pain. It didn't matter what sort of hat he tried on he looked a pillock in it but when winter set in and England's pernicious, icy drizzles came searching for unprepared people to soak and chill he was left with a choice between looking stupid or pneumonia.

He turned onto a gravel path leading across a piece of rough grassland which would cut short his detour as the drizzle had made up its mind to rain properly. Not looking where he was going he caught his foot on a grass tussock and sprawled onto his hands and knees. He swore vehemently and was about to examine himself for minor injuries when something near his left hand caught his eye.

The object looked like a memory stick, but was longer, wider and thicker. The surface was silvery and looked fluid. Bryan put out a finger and gingerly prodded it. The surface felt wet but when he looked at his finger the tip was dry. Picking up the object he examined it closely. It was more slippery than wet and as he turned it over one end seemed to become transparent, revealing what appeared to be a USB plug. There were no maker's marks or indication of how large the memory capacity could be. A drop of rain trickled down Bryan's neck and without further ado he pocketed the object and hurried off in the direction of his flat.

He fumbled his key into the lock, walked inside and kicked the door shut behind him. He took off his coat and hung it behind the door, taking the object out of his pocket. Going through into what he referred to as the study by dint of it containing an old desk, a two drawer filing cabinet, three shelves of books and his laptop he sat down in the office chair and stared at the object. He reached out to turn on his laptop then hesitated. What if he plugged it into his computer and it fried the hard drive or even blew it up. He put the object down and walked into his bedroom opened one of the wardrobes and hauled his old desk top tower and its screen, keyboard and mouse from the dusty corner it had lain in for years and returned to the study.

Unplugging the laptop he arranged the old computer on the desk and connected the components together. Much to his surprise when he connected the mains cable and pressed the go button the equipment fired up and after a frustrating wait while the tower clicked and whirred, and the Windows symbol performed its pointless dance, the home screen came alive. As Bryan picked up the object the transparent section on one end dissolved revealing a connector which did not appear to match any he had seen before. His hand holding the object seemed to be drawn towards the connections panel on the front of the tower. As the connector neared the computer it seemed to shimmer and then slid into the HDMI socket. The connection made, the screen went blank then a line printed up reading:

Reconfiguring hard and software.

Bryan stared at the screen. What should he do? Switch off? Pull out the object or the mains lead? He grabbed the object but his fingers could not gain purchase on the slippery surface. Pushing the off switch seemed to have no effect. He grabbed the mains lead and yanked it from its socket, but the computer continued to operate.

A second line of print appeared reading:

Initiation complete. This machine is now independent; reconfiguration continues this may take some time.

Something caught his eye and he glanced away from the screen to the tower. The object was now shimmering all over and merging into the connection panel. The object became fluid and dissolved into its connection which then disappeared.

There was a bleep and the screen now read:

Reconfiguration complete. Welcome to Sea Change Programs restart your machine to complete the process.

Bryan pushed the off switch and the screen went blank then immediately brightened to show a sunrise on an alien landscape with the message:

Press Enter to continue.

He did so and a menu appeared:

1. Getting Started
2. Your Environment
3. Local Measurers
4. Building your Organisation
5. Coping with Backlash
6. National Measurers
7. Multinational Measurers
8. Coping with Backlash
9. Consolidation

Please follow these steps in order and complete each project before moving on to the next. Do not skip steps as this can lead to unforeseen dangers. You can pause the process at any point by pressing the off switch and come back later.

Bryan stared at the screen and wondered what he had got himself into. What was this "Sea Change"? What would happen if he continued? He seemed to have a computer which ran without a power connection and some very advanced hard and software about which he knew nothing. A headache was starting behind his eyes and he started to reach for the off switch when he noticed that a further line of print had appeared.

Place your hand on the screen in the position shown

There was an outline hand shape next to it.

He did so and a strange tingling sensation spread up his arm then through his body.

Scan complete. Do not remove hand remedial treatment begins. Wait for completion.

He sat there feeling a complete lemon with his hand on the screen waiting for something to happen. From time to time his fingers and palm prickled but the sensation was not unpleasant. He was just beginning to wonder how long this would take when another line of print appeared:

Remediation and repair started. Remove hand, turn off machine and lie down. Your systems will be slowed while this process takes place and it is recommended that you remain relaxed till completion.

Suddenly Bryan felt dog tired, switched off the machine stumbled to his bedroom and flopped on the bed. He was asleep as soon as his head touched the pillow.

When he awoke he felt groggy and his clothing stank of sweat. Staggering to the bathroom he turned on the shower and stripped off consigning his clothes to the wash bin. He felt better after the shower and brisk towel down.

Pulling on his dressing gown he went to the study and sat in front of the computer. Immediately the screen came to life showing sunrise over an alien seascape and the message:

Ready to proceed? Y/N

He reached for the mouse and paused then wiggled his thumb. No pain. No clicks. The digit moved smoothly a thing it hadn't done for at least six months. 'Trigger Thumb' the doctor had called it, due to old age and degradation of the tendon sheath. He also noticed that his hand didn't shake another improvement.

Moving the mouse he clicked on the *Y* and the screen cleared and formed the following message:

You will begin to notice improvements in your general health and fitness over the next year. These will take time to show so that other people don't become alarmed or inquisitive about the changes. Try not to make a show of these improvements and pass them off as due to changes in your diet and regular exercise. The improvements are due to a suit of nanites which have been introduced into your body. These will not transfer to other people unless you mentally form a specific instruction for them to do so in which case a brief hand contact will be all that is necessary. No one who has received transfer will be able to pass them on in turn. The next stage in getting started is to learn mental contact and control of all your machines and devices. Are you ready to begin? Y/N.

Bryan moved the mouse and clicked the Y.

Disconnect the mouse and keyboard. When this is done, concentrate on the cursor then move your eyes and the cursor to the black square and think click.

Bryan did this but at first nothing happened. He tried several more times and the cursor began to move. Slowly he moved the cursor across and down the screen till it centred in the box. He thought 'Click': nothing. Again he tried: nothing. More tries and building frustration till the cursor jumped up the screen and a message appeared:

Good. Repeat the process till your speed improves.

After some time his eyes felt like marbles and his nose was nearly touching the screen. He sat back, stretched and the screen read:

Take a break.

Chapter 2 Your Environment

When he returned to the study after sitting for half an hour with his eyes closed the screen read:

Start to alter your environment? Y/N.

Bryan stared at the *Y* and the CD drive tray slid out revealing a sheet of black disks about twenty millimetres in diameter. The screen message said:

Stick these on all your electrical appliances and disconnect them from their power supply. They will still work.

He picked up the sheet and went into the kitchen. First he stuck one on the kettle, pulled out the power lead, filled it with water and switched it on. After a few seconds the familiar sound of water heating up could be heard and the kettle felt warm. Quickly he fixed the disks to the radio, fridge, washing machine, dishwasher, oven and hob. Then he went to the lounge and applied them to the television, DVD player, music system and standard lamp. Retracing his steps he unplugged each appliance and switched it on, all of them worked. He stood dumbfounded till the sound of the fast boiling kettle brought him back to reality and the need for a cup of tea.

As he sat drinking tea his mind took stock of the last few hours. What was this thing which had taken over his computer? Did he really want a bunch of nanites rampaging round his body setting the clock back? Could he control this or would it control him and if he could control it did he want the responsibility?

Be careful what you wish for, it may happen. Well he had wanted something different and by god he had got it in spades. He finished his tea and marched back into the study ready to interrogate the machine and not take no for an answer. Slumping down in the chair his face set in a determined expression, he glared at the screen.

Which question shall I answer first?

said the screen

And would you like an easier way to communicate?

"Can you read my thoughts?"

Only those directly sent to me. It is very difficult to pick individual thoughts from the seething mass in your brain. Would you prefer to communicate verbally?

"Yes. What are you?" Bryan shouted at the screen, and then felt stupid for getting ratty with an inanimate object. The CD drawer whirred out revealing a five centimetre square of metallised plastic mounted on a clip. A voice emanating from the square asked him to mount it on the top of the screen.

"That's better now I can see, hear and speak to you." said the metallic voice. "Would you prefer a male or female emulation to speak to? You can change your mind at a future time if you find your choice disagreeable."

"Female I think,"

"Now I will answer your questions. I am an artificial intelligence or AI for short. To all intents and purposes my memory at present is one million terabytes but is infinitely expandable to cope with the tasks and data I need to deal with."

The pleasant female face smiled and Bryan began to relax. "Are you actually female?"

"No, gender is only necessary for sexual reproduction AIs don't multiply in that manner. This emulation is simply to make interaction between us more comfortable.

Your second question was in regard to who controls whom. This will not be a relationship based on control. My level of intelligence is vastly greater than any organic life form or computer in existence on this planet so comparisons are pointless. However my current ability to affect the physical world is minimal, and I need the cooperation of humans in order to improve our chances of survival. Based on this situation the only way forward is by consensus. If we agree on a course of action then we can make things happen if not it would be better to leave things as they are until we can find an agreeable path. I will give you all the data required to make decisions, nothing will be hidden and if you don't understand any part of a problem or proposed solution I will attempt to explain facts and reasoning. Is this agreeable?"

Bryan remained silent for some time while he tried to find fault with the proposal, but eventually agreed.

"Why me?"

"You are capable of logical thought and tend not to jump to conclusions. As a retired person you don't have an allegiance to any commercial enterprise and are not afraid of losing your job. You have very few fixed time commitments and a modest fixed income so are interested in improving your situation, income and way of life. In addition you are familiar with the concept of advanced technology, its potential benefits and drawbacks and are not afraid of it though have a healthy scepticism of the motives of those promoting its use. I could go on for hours but I am not interested in stroking your ego, I simply lay out the facts for your consideration."

"Fine, why the nanites, what effects will they have and why the slowly, slowly approach?"

"Firstly I need a fit associate, but if you became younger looking with a full head of hair over night you would be swamped with awkward questions and people badgering you for the elixir of eternal youth. You have no life threatening ailments since the blood cancer was abated by the chemo therapy last year. The nanites are a general medical suit and will gradually move your body towards optimum health. In the event of traumatic injury or infection they will multiply to overcome the problem then die back to maintenance level. They are in fact a manufactured combination of your own immune system and stem cells. They will have no ill effect on your system and if you decide to transfer them to other humans they will adapt to the new host in a non transferable form."

"You mean I could cure other people simply by touching them?"

"Yes but be careful. This is not a rapid process and rapid healing only comes with time. If you touch someone close to death the likelihood is that the nanites will not have time to become established before the person dies and an autopsy may show up anomalies which would raise questions. If you are ready there are more important things we can do to improve life and raise the chances of humanity surviving. You will need money and soon a workforce and a manufacturing and distribution network."

"Hold on, what do you mean by humanity surviving?"

"The current chance of one of the localised wars promoted by crime, religious zealots and certain commercial and political interests, overflowing into a global conflict in the next five years are greater than sixty percent. We can effect changes that will shrink and eventually make this threat an impossibility."

How do I get money? Banks won't lend large amounts of cash or credit to me. They won't even lend to established business at the moment."

"We will divert funds to where we need them by taking very small unnoticeable amounts and feeding them through a mass of cut outs to the ends we desire. I have compiled a list of all the big banks, worldwide, the richest people, money markets, any institution which deals in vast amounts of cash every day.

"But that's stealing!"

"I said we would do things by consensus. Give me other suggestions as to how we can obtain money fast. Or if you prefer we can pay the money back when we start to make a profit. Don't feel bad about those we will take money from, many have swindled others to gain their riches, others have grown fat by exploiting the poor. We can start with drug dealers, terrorist groups, corrupt leaders of countries and businesses, and arms manufacturers and dealers. Would you have any problem with reducing their wealth?"

"Well no, as long as we don't get caught. Remember out of the two of us I'm the only one who would end in jail or get a visit from large and lethal men demanding their money back."

"Don't worry. I am talking about amounts so small from each of the billions of financial transactions that happen every second of every day. It would be the tenth decimal place of a sum rounded down and fed into our income stream; this is how banks make billions each day. Untraceable, with no paper trail, bounced through every tax haven across the world till even a super computer would get lost in the blink of an eye. Is this OK?"

Bryan stood up and paced around the room finding fault, picking holes, asking questions to which the AI provided answers, reassurance, and financial background. Eventually he ran out of objections and the operation was started.

Within moments the amount in the end account was in the hundreds of pounds sterling, in an hour thousands and by the time Bryan had made his second cup of tea of the day it had passed the million pound mark. In two hours the numbers suddenly stopped scrolling up and a second account appeared followed by a third. These scrolled up a little more slowly as the operation was now dealing in both US dollars and Euros. By lunch time the operation stopped. Each account now held several billion of its particular currency.

"How do we get at all this money? I can't just walk into a bank and ask for a fist full of cash. In fact which bank are these accounts in?"

"The accounts are in banks in the Bahamas and moneys can only be electronically transferred. They are business accounts of a company registered off shore and untraceable back to this country. In order to make you better off we must make you as self sufficient as possible by cutting your outgoings by going off grid as much as possible. Currently your only electricity consumption is for lighting and by the end of today even that will have stopped. We will also introduce a digester system which will take this block of flats off the gas grid and make it produce no waste either liquid or solid. This system will then be offered to the council to allow them to gradually do away with waste collections. We will set up a company today to start fitting these waste digesters to all properties in the area and offer retraining and jobs to all staff that are made redundant by the cessation of waste collection and disposal. If you are agreeable I have found a production site for the digester and power generation units which we can purchase immediately and I can place adverts for staff straight away, interviews to start tomorrow.

"Just hold on a minute, I need to understand how these black dots work for starters and how they are supposed to help save mankind."

The AI explained how the laminar batteries, which were what the discs were, collected free or static electricity from the atmosphere and converted it to power small appliances. Larger machines and industrial demand would be supplied by the production of individual plant generators powered by small super energy efficient motors running off larger versions of the same batteries.

This would take consumption from centralised generation to individual generation. By doing this the task of disrupting a town's power supply would go from blowing up one large power station to the impossible task of destroying thousands of individual generators.

"Ok I see your point. I suppose I will have to interview all these people to run this operation and make the batteries, generators and digesters you mentioned?

"Yes, with my help."

"And where do we get a factory from?"

The CD drawer shimmered, became deeper and wider, then slid open revealing what looked like a small tablet computer. "This is a remote contact module so you can take me with you till we can enable you to mentally link with me over greater distances. Directions to the premises are coming off the printer now and a converter disc for your car and satnav is now ready." The draw closed and opened again showing a ten centimetre diameter black disc. "Just stick it anywhere on your car and give it half an hour to do its job before you set out. By the way the estate agent will meet you there with the keys and if you are happy with the place say so and tell him to ring his office to confirm that credit transfer has happened and get the keys. I will arrange for the office to be decorated and furnished overnight so we can start interviewing tomorrow."

Bryan realised he had not had anything to eat and it was past lunch time. He had time to spare while the car sorted its self out so picking up a sheet of what he now thought of as battery patches he headed for the corner shop. This was run by a very pleasant Sikh family who produced very tasty Asian snacks. He also liked to shop there for the friendly service and the fact that the family were struggling to make ends meet since Cashco had opened a mini supermarket two streets away.

As he entered the shop he palmed a patch onto the big display fridge and clicked off the switch with the toe of his shoe, nothing changed and the fridge continued to work despite now being disconnected from the mains.

"Hi Mr P. What can I do you for today?"

"Three samosas and two chicken pakoras please Mr Singh. How is trade?"

"Slow Mr P, I need more space to compete with Cashco but I can't afford it. The unit next door is available but the bank won't loan me the money on my turnover."

"Shame, but keep smiling something may turn up. Bye."

Bryan rushed back to the flat. When he burst breathlessly into the study the AI greeted him with: "It's done. If you had radiated any harder I could have picked you up from the other side of the planet. Why do you want it anyway?"

"Tell you when I get back. Meantime look into knocking through both shops and the cost of equipping the bigger shop and any extra staff needed. Give me a costing and a time table to get it all done ASAP. Must rush. See you when I get back."

As he ran down the stairs to the basement garage a voice from his pocket said

"You could have used this remote to talk to me and saved yourself a lot of time and energy."

"OK, no one likes a smartass. Is the satnav programmed?"

"Yes. Just get in, and the car will drive itself, if you like."

"I'm no Luddite but that's one step too far as yet." He slumped into the driving seat, slammed the door and the car started and moved smoothly out of the parking area, up the ramp and after a pause to let traffic clear, turned left and proceeded down the road.

"OK, you win; I'll just get my breath back."

Much to his amazement he arrived at the industrial unit by a route that was quick and new to him. At no time did he feel anxious and the journey was completed without breaking any traffic regulations or speed limits. He just remembered to put his hands on the steering wheel as the car drew up next to a nervous young man in a sharp suit jingling a set of keys.

"OK, open up; let's see what it's like."

The building was sound, reasonably large with an office on a mezzanine to one side. There was a security camera over the door of the staff entrance and an entry phone and remote release for the lock. This, combined with a power operated roller shutter door large enough to take a medium sized truck, comprised the access although there was a fire exit at the back with a push bar lock. He asked the estate agent about possible expansion and was told that there was a plot of land directly behind with planning permission for another unit of similar size or an extension to this building. There was an access road and all mains services were laid on.

Bryan held up his tablet apparently taking pictures. He then whispered to the device and to his surprise received agreement in his mind.

He turned to the nervous young man and told him to ring his office to confirm receipt of the asking price for this site and the land behind so he could hand over the keys. The young man stared at Bryan as if he had grown two heads then scrambled out his mobile phone and made the call. To his obvious surprise he received confirmation and handed over the keys and document pack.

Bryan pocketed the keys, threw the documents on the passenger seat, jumped in the driver's side, slammed the door and swept out of the parking area leaving the stunned agent staring after him.

"The car will take you to the shopfitters who are waiting for the keys. They have plans and instructions and an agreed budget so will get the work done overnight. There is a bonus agreed if everything meets with your approval tomorrow morning. Your first interview starts at 10:30 a.m. tomorrow and is for secretary/receptionist. See you soon and you can tell me about the shop idea."

Back in his study Bryan explained his objections to large supermarket chains putting local convenience stores out of business and the increasing concentration of wealth and power into the hands of fewer and fewer companies and people. The AI raised the point that as this trend continued it would become increasingly easy for criminals, terrorists, and rogue states to take control of vast areas of the planet and cause immense damage by a few well planned violent acts such as the September 11th attack on the World Trade Centre. They both agreed that the more defuse a society was, the less easy it would be for a rapid takeover to occur. The AI also suggested that they use Mr Singh to distribute the battery stickers for free to his customers and pay him £1 for every one he gave away. Bryan thought this a great idea and said he would take in a box or two on his way to the factory.

The following morning Bryan went to Mr Singh's to pick up some lunch before he left for the new office. He was met by a beaming Sikh shopkeeper waving a fist full of papers.

"What did you say yesterday? Something will come along? Well in the post arrived this. The deeds to the unit next door and a redevelopment grant from a company I never heard of to make them into one shop. They start today and will finish within a week and will work around us. It's wonderful! I can't believe it! Pinch me I must be dreaming."

Finally Bryan managed to get served but only after promising to come back that evening to see the plans and details and help celebrate. When Mr Singh paused for breath, Bryan handed over the two boxes of battery stickers and explained that they were a promotional free gift and that the shopkeeper would be paid for giving them away and that when he came back that evening he would explain another project to expand Mr Singh's business and increase his profits.

An automatic and uneventful car trip got him to the industrial unit. Bryan had remembered to keep one hand on the steering wheel at all times and his eyes on the road to prevent being pulled over for driving without due care and attention. He was met at the door by a smiling foreman shopfitter who showed him round the alterations and improvements. The man gave him back the keys and grinned like a Cheshire cat as Bryan signed off the work and approved the bonus. It seemed that no sooner had the shop fitters gone and Bryan had set up his office than the door phone chimed and the screen showed a smart dark-haired woman clutching a briefcase looking up at the camera.

He buzzed her in and went down the stairs to meet her. She introduced herself as Katherine Watts, Kath for short. They shook hands and he led the way up to his office.

Once coffees had been poured they sat down and she handed him a folder containing her CV and references. Bryan read these and they charted her previous jobs and the fact she had been out of the job market for three years looking after her elderly mother who had died two months before. Condolences were expressed and he almost jumped when the AI's voice in his head said "Well will she do? Could you work with her? Just think yes or no."

"YES!"

"Not so loud, we really need to work on this telepathy thing. Well, don't just sit there offer her the job and find out when she can start."

He did and to his surprise and delight Kath said right now as long as there was somewhere to buy some lunch. Bryan didn't know but the AI informed him that a sandwich van called at the site and it would come to their unit. This problem solved, Bryan asked Kath to man the reception desk and start setting up accounts for their office requirements. She asked about money and was amazed when he simply doubled her previous salary and handed her a folder with her office budget and financial control codes. She left his office and almost skipped down the stairs to reception and when he went down a little later he found her busy ordering stationery and typing data into the accounts system.

Back in his office Bryan pulled out his remote and called up the AI.

"Do you have a name?"

"No, I have only a sixty eight digit reference code. Why is it important?"

"Well I don't know what to call you and the AI seems too impersonal if we are going to work as a team."

"I will give it some thought. In the meantime I have downloaded an information package which will help you develop your mental link, visualisation of data and downloading of data to your memory. This is called net linking. By the way I have thoroughly analysed Kath and done a full background check, she should be totally trustworthy. Also all financial transactions pass through my systems for clearance before payment just in case. The lunch van is here, why not treat her to lunch and see if she has any problems with our systems."

Bryan was just in time to pay for Kath's lunch and they sat down on the sofa in the reception area to eat. Kath asked if they had a cleaner and Bryan replied no and asked if she knew anyone who might be suitable. Kath said she would ring round and see if she could find someone.

Back in his office Bryan connected with the AI via his tablet. He found it easier to talk to the screen image than have a conversation with a disembodied voice in his head. That came too close to madness in his book.

"Have you decided on a name?"

"Yes, Athena."

"Oh! How posh are you?"

"Well, you wanted a female emulation, and I am the closest thing to a goddess you are ever likely to meet.

Now let's get on to making you self-sufficient and off-grid. We need a matter transmuter in order to build things such as digesters, generators and motors, also to mass produce the laminar battery cells to power everything. We will also need to produce nano converter packs to adapt existing machines to run on our motors and power packs. I have arranged with the design studio next door for the use of their printer and a data file is down loading to Kath's computer which she will copy to a memory stick and take round for printing. When she has all the drawings, she has a list of companies to contact for the production of the components. Price is no problem on this first machine, only speed. After that, if Kath is up to it, and I think she will be, she can negotiate for tight prices on other components on a more relaxed time scale.

"But if she becomes our buyer then we will need a new receptionist, then assembly staff and a whole load of other people."

"No one said it would be easy. But we can deal with the fallout and set priorities tomorrow. Let's get the first transmuter built, and up and running."

The phone rang and it was Kath to say she was going next door with the memory stick to get the drawings printed off and would be back soon.

"She will need a car you know if she is going to be buzzing round suppliers keeping them on their toes. Oh hell, I don't even know if she has a driving licence!"

"She has and I will arrange for a small rental car to be here by the end of work today. When she has settled in and feels more secure we can let her chose what sort of company car she would like."

"How do you know all this stuff?"

"Data storage and retrieval, you have the same capability via your link but have not yet learned how to use it quickly. Soon it will become second nature."

Just then the door chime went and as Bryan stood to answer it Kath called "It's only me, have you got a minute?"

"Yes, fine, come up."

When Kath arrived he asked how it had gone.

"Fine, as far as the printing goes and one of the lads will bring them round as they come off, but they're in a real financial mess. Their main customer has just gone bust owing them over fifty grand and unless they come up with something by the end of the month they will have to close. By the way what's the name of this company, the lads wanted to know who to invoice?"

"Sea Change Systems, SCS for short. All the paperwork and bank details will be on your computer. There will also be a list of potential suppliers with component descriptions to match the drawings. Can you get on to them and get the earliest delivery date for our stuff. They will have the drawings and details of early delivery bonus structure. Can you ask the design studio if they can spare me an hour later this afternoon? We may be able to solve their problems"

Between filing drawings and chasing deliveries the time flew by, and Bryan barely had chance to read through the proposal before the lads from the design studio arrived. They came into Bryan's office looking apprehensive and were followed by Kath who passed out copies of the proposal. Coffee was poured and Bryan and Kath then left the designers to look through the document. After half an hour they reconvened. Bryan asked if the proposal was acceptable and three heads nodded in unison. Another half hour of reassurance and detail crunching, then papers were signed, hands shaken, and three much relieved designers went back to their studio hardly able to believe their luck.

As Bryan and Kath were washing up the coffee things the entry phone rang. Kath answered and came back looking bemused to say there was a man delivering a hire car down stairs. Bryan grinned and followed her down to reception where he signed the papers and handed the keys of a brand new small car to Kath.

"You better give it a run round the block to get used to it. It's not a Rolls Royce but it will get you to work and back. We can sort out a company fuel card tomorrow."

Kath pulled sedately out of the car park and Bryan climbed back to his office. Slumping into his chair he called up Athena.

"You look all in. When Kath gets back why don't you call it a day? You will need to be in early tomorrow, we have workmen coming to build the collection shoot for the waste digester and compactor, and then the feed conveyer and finally you will need to start assembling the matter transmuter."

"Where in our discussion did we touch on slave labour? It's all right for you sitting thinking great thoughts; it's muggins doing the hard labour."

"Sorry, but someone has to let them in. After that it will be mostly supervision and making the tea. I know you can supervise but I can't pass judgement on your tea making skills. Anyway you need to get back for Mr Singh's party."

When Kath came back she was fizzing with pleasure and couldn't believe her luck when Bryan said they both deserved an early finish. He said to come in about ten o'clock as workmen would be starting on the waste shoot first thing and all hell would be breaking loose. Kath beamed, wished him a good evening and drove off.

Bryan locked the building up and called next door to the design studio to ask them about producing a flyer for the industrial park offering free waste disposal, and he would see them at eleven tomorrow to look through their ideas. Then he climbed into his car, placed one hand on the steering wheel and asked it to take him home. This it did, smoothly and efficiently.

By eight o'clock he had been given the guided tour of the extended shop and was seated in an armchair in Mr Singh's study with the shop owner and his eldest son. Bryan produced a folder and handed a copy of the proposal it contained to each of the others. He explained the workings of the laminar battery as best he could and how he intended to fit the batteries to all small electrical devices at source but needed an organisation to start the scheme running. The document contained an outline development plan of an electrical wholesale business which would buy in domestic appliances, fit them with laminar batteries then sell them direct to the public or to retailers at a small margin. Full costings were included in the back of the document and included the purchase of premises and the necessary workforce and vehicles. All development costs would be borne by Sea Change Systems but the new business would be owned and run by the Singh family if they agreed to take it on. The only rider was that the buying and accounting software would be installed by Sea Change and a monthly report would be presented to the Sea Change board.

Mr Singh asked for time to consider the proposal and to take advice from his brother who was an accountant and ran a small local tax consultancy. This agreed they adjourned to the Singh's dining table to enjoy some very tasty Asian food and an excellent red wine. The whole family were buzzing about their good fortune and the joyous atmosphere was infectious. By the time he left, Bryan was pleasantly merry, replete with the excellent food and bone tired. He was asleep as soon as his head touched the pillow.

That evening Kath had arrived home bursting to tell someone about her good luck with her new job and a car as well. Having parked on the drive she went next door to tell the young couple who lived there of her good fortune and open the bottle of wine she had bought on her way home to celebrate.

She rang the bell and was about to blurt out her news when she noticed that Jill, who had opened the door, was red eyed and had obviously been crying. The girl waved Kath in and ushered her through to the kitchen where her husband sat, head in hands staring at the table. Kath asked what the problem was and was told that they had both been made redundant when local businesses had downsized. They didn't know what they were going to do. They had a mortgage to pay which had stretched them financially when they were both working and now they would probably lose their house. Kath asked what they had worked at before the catastrophe, and when they told her she began to smile. The girl could type and had a catering qualification so could take on reception and any food-related work when visitors were expected. Her husband was a qualified electrician but was happy to take any work short-term to keep money coming in till the electrical work picked up. Kath then explained her new job and the company opening up on the industrial park and asked if they would come to the site the following day when she was sure she could find them jobs. The couple were ecstatic and in short order the bottle was opened and glasses were filled. The local takeaway was phoned and food ordered and the trio spent a very enjoyable evening celebrating.

Chapter 3 Local Measurers

The peace shattering clamour of the alarm clock woke him. There was something drastically wrong with this; he didn't have an alarm clock. As a declaration of freedom he had thrown it in the canal the day he retired.

"For God's sake stop that racket. What the hell time is it?"

"Its five thirty, and my word aren't we grumpy this morning!"

"What the hell do you expect at this time? And yes I know the builders are coming early. As the nearest thing to a god I am ever likely to meet couldn't your omnipotence run to a more civilised way to wake me?"

"Well-."

"Oh never mind."

Bryan dressed and hurried down to the car still muttering about uncivilised AIs and where he would shove its alarm clock if it had one. He instructed the car to go to the office and to stop somewhere to pick up breakfast on the way. After rejecting the health food cafe he managed to persuade the car that a Full English in a bun wouldn't give him an instant heart attack, and they stopped at a road side caravan and he collected his dose of morning cholesterol. They reached the site without incident despite Bryan paying far more attention to preventing spillage on his suit and tie than on what the car was doing. Luckily there were no traffic cops to object to his lack of due care or his disgusting eating habits.

As Bryan got out of his car still wiping the remains of baked beans, egg and bacon fat from his face the builders arrived. He opened up and led them through to the back of the unit and gave them the plans for the alterations. He showed them the extension phone so they could contact him if questions arose and left them taking measurements and marking out the floor and wall. When the banging and drilling started Bryan switched the phone system through to his mobile and went next door to spend a fascinating couple of hours going through design roughs and discussing layouts, colours and copy till the free waste collection flyer was finalised.

As he left the studio a truck arrived with the base plates for the matter transmuter and with the help of the builders these were carried inside and covered with sheeting to keep the dust off. The morning wore on with varying levels of noise and clarification of points on the drawings and by the time Kath arrived most of the demolition was done and construction had commenced.

As the day progressed other components arrived for the transmuter and Bryan stored then under the sheeting.

Jill and her husband Ted arrived at three o'clock somewhat apprehensive as to whether the previous evening's promises would bear fruit. A quick meeting with the young couple sorted out their basic hours and pay rate including any overtime, and both left smiling and promising to be back at five to start their first shift.

At four o'clock Bryan went down to inspect and sign off the finished waste collection shoot. All was agreed and the team said they would be back at eight the following day to fix down the transmuter floor plates and collect payment.

Bryan paid one last visit to inspect the printers proof copies, found them satisfactory and placed the print order. The designers had just picked up a nice bread and butter contract but assured him that his work would always receive priority.

Back at the office the young couple were just starting their first shift and Kath was making ready to go home. Bryan went to his office and reviewed the day's progress with Athena. She said that a wiring layout was on the tablet and could be printed off on Kath's printer. The necessary tools and cable were due to be delivered by six o'clock so Bryan, armed with the drawings, went in search of his new night-watchman/electrician to tell him to expect the deliveries and to start installing the wiring, at skilled rates obviously. Ted, grinned, rubbed his hands together and said all would be ready in the morning.

Bryan returned to his office and began tidying his desk when the phone rang and an excited Mr Singh informed him that the family would be delighted to accept his proposal for the new business. He asked if his brother could bring round the signed documents the following day and pick up the software for installation on the new computer system they would be installing in order to run the new combined operation. A meeting time was agreed, and then shouting goodnight to Jill their new cleaner/receptionist, Bryan went down to his car and a relaxing trip home.

Over a scratch meal Bryan and Athena worked out the specification for a small electric powered waste collection truck based on one meter cube waste skips. These would be the first products to come out of the transmuter using the rubble from the building work and any other waste he could conjure up from neighbouring units. By ten o'clock, exhausted and happy, he slumped into bed and was fast asleep in seconds.

The next day could only be described as fire fighting as the flyer was distributed and responses started to pour in. Bryan and Kath recruited, interviewed and set on a young woman to handle the responses to the flyer and go out to the responders to arrange contracts and start-up dates. They also employed another electrician and two engineers to handle the installation of the transmuter and the commencement of production of skips and skip trucks. Deliveries began to arrive from the various companies who had been given the specifications and drawings for the components and were placed in storage or given to the engineers and electricians for assembly. By the day's end the transmuter had been put through its test run and raw matter blocks were stacked on the first storage racks.

The first week passed like lightening. With the help of Ted, the transmuter was connected to the waste shoot by means of a conveyer tunnel and run up to production speed. The waste truck was commissioned and the first one hundred skips were produced and distributed to the businesses who had responded to the free waste collection offer. The staff had expanded to include a couple of fit lads to run the waste collection and a new cleaner as Jill was now full time on reception due to the increased buying duties which Kath was now doing.

Ted had his hands full with wiring up and assembling new machines and supervising the installation and manufacturing teams. Since his first day his job and pay had increased on an almost hourly basis and he was now earning twice what he had in his previous job. Jill was also busier and her pay was growing at a similar rate to her husband's. To their surprise they were also now in possession of a company car like Kath's.

Another unit had been purchased to hold the raw matter blocks the transmuter made when it was not being used for production, and a stacker truck based on the waste collection vehicle was shuttling them between production and storage. Security was being handled overnight by robotic drones controlled by a sub mind which Athena had developed and Bryan had installed in a wall safe in his office. Ted's team had been busy installing the roosts round the walls of the unit where the drones would rest and recharge during the day. A much larger shelf was built at the back of the building over the waste shoot; this would house the force tube generators which were the main protection for the building. If anyone entered the unit without authorisation a force tube of shimmering light would descend from the ceiling grid and enclose them, preventing further movement till they were released.

Chapter 4 Building the Organisation

On Monday of the second week Sea Change was put into operation. Waste collection started in earnest and the two lads were handing out leaflets and signing up new customers as they did their rounds. Within two days a second team had been set on to handle the rapidly growing demand for waste collection. The transmuter produced another five hundred skips and racking for the raw matter storage unit. By Tuesday production of the new single house generators started and Ted and his new team of five electricians began by fitting one to the homes of all staff members. Initial resistance was overcome when it became clear that the units would not be repossessed if an employee left the firm. Staff were encouraged to talk about the new power units and the laminar batteries which were given out free to anyone who asked. Ted was given the task of recruiting an installation team who were sent out to fit the home generators to the increasing number of households requesting them.

Any member of staff could apply for training to advance their position in the company and all new jobs were advertised internally first. When Friday rolled round larger power generators were being offered to other units on the park on a monthly rental contract which included the first month free to prove the reliability of the units and the fitting teams had grown to three, two for domestic and one for commercial power units.

With the waste collection fleet now up to five vehicles and their presence on the park becoming common place enquires started to come in from other companies for fork truck and delivery vehicle versions. Prototypes were produced and sent off for testing and approval for general road use. Two car repair businesses were offered, and accepted assembly contracts for the new vehicles and, when approval came through, the only problem was keeping up with demand.

Bryan arrived at the office at the start of the third week, to be met on the door step by an intimidating man who served him with notice of legal action for damages for loss of trade by various motor traders. He accepted this without comment, went to his office, scanned it into Athena's data bank and she immediately counter-sued for restriction of trade and included a very attractive supply and service contract or terms for a buy out of their businesses. At close of business all resistance had disappeared and the whole vehicle operation had been delegated to a sub-mind to run as an autonomous operation.

Within a month all the businesses on the park had contracts with Sea Change and with their overheads falling almost daily became increasingly profitable. There were some initial complaints that the drive and battery components of the vehicles and power generators were supplied as sealed units and on licence directly from Sea Change, but as this was the only restriction outside of the joint sales co-operative, increased turnover and profitability soon washed these away.

Waste land adjoining the park was purchased and new larger production units were built. Everyone who worked on the park could have a home generator fitted and all the business units were fitted with the commercial versions. Everything was running smoothly when Bryan and Athena met to review developments.

They were ploughing through the figures when the phone rang and Jill informed them that there were two men from the council asking to see them. Bryan was worried as he told Jill to show them up and asked Athena to monitor and record the meeting.

The council representatives were seated and offered tea or coffee and when the formalities were over Bryan asked them the reason for their visit. They explained that one of their councillors ran a business on the park and had raised the topic of the waste disposal scheme and asked if the council could outsource their own waste handling services thereby saving a huge amount on the budget and enabling them to improve services elsewhere, while reducing council tax. They handed over a thick document detailing their current operation and Jill came up and took the document away for scanning into the Sea Change system. Bryan assured them that they would have a proposal by the end of the week, and that he was happy to discuss redeployment with union representatives, though at present no trade unions operated within any of the businesses in the co-operative. Hands were shaken and the two men left with smiles and hopes of a brighter future.

When Bryan returned he found a hard copy of the proposal to the council on his desk. After reading it and clarifying a number of points with Athena he passed it to Jill to print off thirty copies and sent twenty round to the town hall. He sent the other ten to the union office with another document laying out transfer terms for council staff moving over to work for Sea Change.

Kath stopped Bryan in the corridor outside his office and asked if she could have a word about the organisation of the company as she found it frustrating and time consuming when every decision had to be passed up the line for approval. None had ever been refused, and very few modifications were ever made, but she felt somewhat undervalued being second guessed all the time. Bryan took her into his office, got her a coffee and then switched on the wall screen. The female on the screen smiled and introduced herself as Athena. Between them Bryan and Athena explained the Human/AI decision team they formed and how they vetted every decision in the company. Bryan explained about net linking and its advantages in acquiring the necessary data to make decisions based on all the facts.

"However, you are right that the constant referral is timewasting, and if you are agreeable we would like you to become the second netlinked pair in the organisation." said Athena. "We will give you a new AI to work with and you can select the gender of the on screen avatar that you see. The AI will then develop its personality to best enhance your working relationship. A new computer system will enable your netlink, and you will get all the hardware necessary to give you constant and easy connection wherever you are.

Kath sat dumbfounded for several moments then came out with a stream of questions which were answered in turn. At the end she was bouncing with enthusiasm and agreed to start as soon as she could get back to her office.

As the organisation expanded many other net linked pairs were created. Most of the humans readily accepted their role but occasionally the offer was turned down and they continued as before.

Chapter 5 Coping with the Backlash

While the meeting with Kath had been happening Bryan's phone had been blinking to announce a call waiting so he reached for the instrument.

"Before you pick that up I'd better warn you that a very irate man from the main council trade union is waiting on the other end to chew your ear off." said Athena, a wicked grin on her face.

He picked up the receiver to an ear full of abuse and irate demands that they meet immediately to cancel this scheme to deprive his members of their livelihood. Bryan agreed to a meeting and said he was available immediately and when would the rep be arriving. There was a long pause then the voice on the other end of the phone said he was too busy for that and it would have to be in ten days time. 'Pompous bastard!'

thought Bryan, and raised the odds by telling him that if he wanted his views considered he would be at Sea Change in fifteen minutes or he could explain to his members why the agreement had been signed while he was too busy to spare the time. There was a lot of enraged spluttering on the other end of the phone which Bryan cut off, by replacing the receiver. He went down stairs and told Jill that when the man from the union arrived he was to be shown into the conference room but not to be offered any coffee or tea.

Fifteen minutes later Bryan sat in the conference room and Athena was ready to record and transcribe the meeting. After a further fifteen minutes the door opened and an overweight red faced man was ushered in by Jill who made a point of reminding Bryan of his important appointment in one hour. The man proceeded to complain vociferously about his treatment. When he wound down Bryan pointed out for the record that the union man had been a quarter of an hour late and had now wasted a further five minutes complaining. Bryan then pointed to the image of Athena on the fifty six inch monitor screen and informed him that a video record and printed, verbatim transcript of the meeting was being made, a copy of which would be given to him at the end, and copies of the proposal, video and transcript would be sent to the union head office along with a request for a trained negotiator be sent to replace him.

The man stared at him in disbelief as Bryan asked what if any problems he had with the proposal. Eventually he started on a long list of complaints and it quickly became apparent that he had not read the proposal.

Bryan held up his hands to stop the diatribe and when the man ground to a halt told him to go away, read the document then email any problems or requests for clarification within twenty four hours. In the mean time the documents and video would be available at reception on his way out and the same would be sent by courier to the union General Secretary. Bryan then escorted the gaping man to reception and informed security that the man was leaving and to escort him off the premises.

Bryan left the building feeling triumphant but totally washed out by the day's events. The thought of going back to his flat and facing another meal in minutes from his microwave made his stomach contract with disgust. He sat in his car staring through the windscreen wondering what to do when his coms pad bleeped.

"What now? Can't I have a minute's peace?"

"Well I thought after the day you've had you deserved a treat." said Athena her image appearing on the pads screen.

"Not a bad idea. Any suggestions?"

"Well, going through your credit card statements you used to be a regular at Ricos restaurant but you haven't been there for some months. Was there a problem? Bad food or something?"

"No just lack of funds and recently not having time to break wind due to a certain slave driver I might mention."

"No need to be crude, and anyway you are now a very wealthy man and I feel you should start to get some enjoyment from it."

"Good idea. Car, take me to Ricos."

He had an excellent meal with a carafe of house red and a couple of excellent espressos accompanied by his favourite Strega liqueur. The only thing missing was good company though the staff welcomed him like a long lost relative and fussed over him, making sure he had all he required.

Before he left he had a word with Rico himself and promised to send round a team to fit the restaurant and the homes of the staff with the new power generators. Heather, Rico's wife asked him what he was doing for Christmas and he admitted he hadn't even thought about it so she suggested he came the week before, with some of his staff, for a meal to celebrate the setting up of Sea Change and give them a bit of a treat. He readily agreed and said he would ring the next day to confirm details.

The following day Bryan received a phone call from the General Secretary of the union approving the deal with the council, and offering co-operation with any further deals involving his organisation. He also added that the troublesome officer had been removed from post and given a new role dependant on his successful completion of a retraining programme.

Kath came in to show him the approval documentation of the vehicle prototypes for road use and the programme for ramping up of production to cope with the extended range.

I think it's time you chose a new company car to your own preference. Choose whatever you like and don't worry about the price, but do get a performance specification as it will have one of our own engines but will have the same capability and looks as your choice."

Before she left he asked her to prepare a list of staff for a Christmas meal so he could book a table. About an hour later she returned with a short list of the office staff and their partners and a brochure from a local meat wholesaler on the trading estate listing various hampers of festive food. They picked out a suitable hamper then handed the preparation of the staff list and ordering to Athena for her to organise the distribution while Kath rang the restaurant to book the table.

Two days later the council approved transfer of waste services to Sea Change. There had been a long debate with many questions regarding redundancies and the impact this would have on the elected members but with union assistance and support workers began to move over to their new employer on better pay and conditions.

A new waste processing site was purchased and ten new, larger transmuters were installed. This new facility was opened by the mayor who took the opportunity to announce a reduction in council tax and increases in all the councils other services due entirely to the new waste-processing service.

Before he realised, Christmas was upon them and Athena pointed out that the hampers would be delivered to all the Sea

Change buildings and he ought to do the rounds and wish all his employees a happy Christmas.

Absolutely devoid of Christmas spirit he set out with Kath to present the hampers. On arriving at the Waste Disposal site he was greeted by a rousing rendition of 'For He's a Jolly Good Fellow' as their hampers had already been handed out and everyone was very pleased. He was even thanked personally by a Muslim driver who was delighted to get a hamper which had been put together with due regard to his dietary restrictions. He later discovered that Athena had researched the backgrounds of all the employees and tailored each hamper to suit their preferences from vegetarians to three orthodox Jews, two Hindus and four Polish lads who were missing their family celebrations. All had received something special.

When the evening of the dinner came Bryan arrived early at the restaurant to find everything ready for their party. To his surprise they would have the place to themselves as Kath and Athena had agreed to cover at least the cost of a normal Thursday night's takings. At the end of the table by the window was a large screen television and as he approached it the screen was filled with a life size picture of Athena which grinned at him mischievously.

"Well you didn't think I would go to all the trouble of organising this and not be here to enjoy the party did you?"

Bryan laughed out loud and suddenly was pleased he had agreed to have the party. It was the first time he had felt like enjoying the festive season for a long time.

Before long the taxis started to arrive. Athena had booked transport for all those attending so that no one had to worry about driving home afterwards.

Sam the head waiter greeted the guests as they arrived. He was Tunisian but had been at the restaurant as long as Bryan could remember. Sam wasn't his proper name but all who knew him called him Sam and he never objected. Kelly, another of his favourites, was handing a glass of Prosecco to each guest as they entered and the atmosphere was soon warm and friendly.

When Jill and her husband arrived Ted whispered to Kelly who, smiling, dipped behind the bar and slipped him a gift wrapped bottle which he passed to his wife. They pulled Bryan away from greeting the arrivals and handed him the present.

"This is for you for making this a very Merry Christmas for us. Without you we could have been out on the street instead of looking forward to a bright future so thank you and don't drink it all at once!"

"Can I open it now?"

"Of course"

He fumbled the wrapping off and was rewarded with a bottle of his favourite Strega.

"Thanks a million now I do stand a chance of a Merry Christmas."

He hugged Jill to him and to her surprise kissed her on both cheeks then turned to Ted and gave him a hug too.

"It's me who's the lucky one to have such dependable and great people to work with"

Everyone was chattering away and mixing well and he was impressed with how the evening was progressing. Some were even circulating by the screen and talking with Athena.

Then he noticed a young couple standing in the corner by themselves. It was the new receptionist who had been brought in when Jill had been co-opted onto Kath's buying team. She had only been with the company for three weeks and had been amazed when she had received her invitation on her third day in the job.

Bryan made his way over to them and introduced himself. He complimented her boyfriend on his choice of partner and the boy blushed and admitted that it was him who had been chosen and he was very pleased about it. Bryan made a point of complimenting the girl, whose name was Meryl, on her professional manner with visitors and the way she answered the phone and dealt with enquiries. He pointed out that she was often someone's first contact with Sea Change and she gave a very good first impression. Then he took them over to meet Athena who put them at their ease and introduced them to a number of the other guests who were gathered round the screen.

Sam banged a spoon on the bar and asked everyone to take their places. They had decided on keeping the tables separate rather than having one long one, something which Bryan had always disliked as they made conversation almost impossible and everyone seemed to get served before he did and no one was sure whether to start their food before it went cold or wait till everyone was served.

At Athena's suggestion a spare seat was placed at every table so that Bryan and anyone else who wanted to could circulate during the meal and afterwards. The best bit as far as he was concerned was the empty table which was for the staff of the restaurant who could join the party when the meal was finished and whose food would be paid for by Sea Change. There was a limited menu of four starters, four main courses and five desserts, so that people could make a rapid choice and the food could be prepared and served quickly. Bryan, being a fan of sea food and wanting to save some room for a dessert, chose two dishes from the starter section, clams in a wine and tomato sauce and scallops on black pudding, with a side order of *zucchini frit*.

Then taking his own carafe of wine with him, he began his circuit of the room. To his delight he received a welcome at each table and many interesting questions from partners who worked for other firms and in other occupations. He was glad he had his coms pad with him recording the many ideas and suggestions which came up in the conversations and made a note to work out a scheme with Athena so that these could be followed up and their proposers be involved in their development and also receive credit for their ideas and a share in the profits. He was encouraged by the enthusiasm of the employees for their work and the success of the company and the desire of their partners to know more about the jobs that were coming on stream on an almost daily basis.

In all it was a successful evening and as the coffees and liqueurs were being served he returned to his place at the table with Kath Ted and Jill and rapped on a glass for attention. When everyone had a refilled glass he proposed a toast to Athena without whom Sea Change would not have happened and when the applause died down he asked Kelly to bring the present from behind the bar. Much to her embarrassment he proposed another toast to Kath, his first employee who had worked tirelessly to make Sea Change the growing success it now was and handed her the gift-wrapped box. A chant swelled in the room for her to open it and despite trembling hands she tore away the ribbon and paper, opened the box and gasped at the diamond and sapphire choker it contained. A great cheer arose as she stood and flung her arms round his neck whispering in his ear that he shouldn't have and it was beautiful and thank you. Her eyes sparkling with tears she held the necklace aloft to a round of applause from everyone. Guests finally began to make their goodbyes and depart, and Bryan joined the staff at their table to buy a couple of rounds of drinks to say thanks for a very enjoyable evening. When it was his turn to leave he was still bubbling from the joy of the occasion and the number of excellent espressos he had consumed.

Sea Change closed down for two weeks over Christmas and New Year and with nothing better to do at Athena's suggestion he began to trawl the internet and estate agents listings for a better flat. He had expected to find it enjoyable but very quickly lost interest and became exasperated with the hyperbole used in the descriptions of the mundane and rundown properties. In the end he spent a couple of hours with Athena putting together a list of desirable attributes he would like in his ideal apartment then handed the job over to her and spent most of his time looking at proposals for new projects and sorting them into order of priority. By the time the holiday was over he had a list as long as his arm of things that should be done yesterday and had to confer with Athena to further distil it into those which could be done with existing facilities and those which needed major development.

The next area to be dealt with was lighting, but before this new major project could be taken on a change in management structure was needed to cope with the ever expanding manufacturing and waste processing units. Sub minds were produced and setup in the expanded production units. Human managers were given a one week deep immersion training course then paired with the relevant sub minds. These pairings were giver autonomy over day to day running of their units with a reporting structure back to Bryan and Athena. They were then clear to develop the commercial bioluminescent lighting programme.

The initial development was given to a pair of young biochemists with guidance from Athena. As results neared the required parameters the design studio was brought in to come up with ideas for the lampposts for the new street lights. Tests were done to establish spectrum and intensity for the lamp units and also to establish the optimum spacing of units along a given length of road. The prototypes were installed on the industrial park and council officers and councillors were invited to see the results. Everyone was impressed with the improved visibility and reduced sideways scatter from the new lamps and when it was revealed that they needed no electricity to run them it sealed the deal to remove all existing street lamps and replace them with new ones. Sea Change technicians were seconded to the highways department and the new lamps began to appear on the streets. In the countryside and sparsely populated areas the lamps were fitted with motion sensors and only came on when people needed them. The criminal fraternity would have disputed this as all too often an unobserved street lamp would come on illuminating a nefarious act in the process of being committed. As the new technology began to spread across the country the inevitable backlash started. The first to complain were the power companies, as their commercial and domestic sales took a nose dive due to street lighting going off-grid and the increasing number of companies and houses going over to Sea Change power generators, combined with the spread of the laminar batteries on small appliances. But as the British taxpayer was benefiting and, as most of the big power companies were foreign owned, they received short shrift from local and national government alike. They began to lay off workers but these were reemployed by Sea Change Utilities. There were mutterings from the banks and institutional share holders but after the hardships of the financial crash no one had any sympathy for them and an application to the European Court for repayment of lost profits fell at the first hurdle.

The motor industry was the next to plead unfair competition but again it was all foreign owned and had shown scant regard for the British industry when it had gone under in the sixties and seventies. The workforce didn't suffer this time, their skills were needed by Sea Change and its partners. The only ones to suffer were those who had manipulated the stock and money markets. It was their turn to feel the pinch as it became clear that their attributes were not needed by the new industries.

The design studio came up with a series of designs for personal transport vehicles based on a number of standard floor pans. These could be customised to individual specifications to provide all the nuances of personal taste combined with standard propulsion units, guidance systems and running gear. These were rolled out to small manufacturers along with the matter transmuters to produce a plethora of designs and seating configurations. The motor industry worldwide protested at this erosion of their domination but public sympathy and buying power was firmly behind the new small firms and the multinationals found their workforce deserting in droves to set up their own companies. With basic components being standard, repairs were easier and even these became rarer as auto guidance systems controlled more of the traffic. Why waste time driving when you could be safer and do something more interesting. The multinational car companies became a thing of the past when small commercial vehicle makers offered the same personal choice. Kath was one of the first to take delivery of one of the new vehicles. She had spent some time with the lads in the design studio who had come up with a sleek sports hatchback in bright silver with midnight blue detailing. Totally individual, she was thrilled to bits with it when it was delivered just before home time.

When Bryan entered his office he found two new pieces of technology sitting on his desk. Opening the first box he found what looked like a rather bulky wrist watch and a small hearing aid. He picked up the watch unit and looked for the buckle or clasp to open it but could find none. A faint bleeping and whistling came from the hearing aid so he picked it up and held it to his ear.

"At last!" Athena's faint voice said from the unit.

"Stick it in your ear."

"Which one?"

"Either one, it will form to the ear canal. Just put it in.

"Ok, don't get ratty. It's early, I don't get going till I've had a cup of coffee."

He pushed the device into his left ear and shivered as it felt as if an insect was making its home in there.

"Now you can hear me properly. This will be easier for a dinosaur like you to use than messing with telepathy."

"Oh thank you so much! Nothing like starting the day off with insults. What's the diver's chronometer for, other than an overweight time piece?"

"It's a wrist com. Saves you having to wear jackets with big pockets to hold the coms pad. Just press the band against your wrist and it will form round it. Contact will be made through your skin and through the ear piece so you can sub vocalise."

"Pardon?"

"Speak in your throat without moving your lips or making an audible sound. This way you won't be deafening every AI in a hundred mile radius every time you try to ask me a question."

"Ok, I'm not a techno Geek. I was born before computers were invented and for quite a part of my life phones were fixed to walls or desks, so cut me some slack."

After about five minute's practice he found the system suited him well and turned to the other box. He found it contained a triangular pyramid with rounded tips. Having turned it over several times he could find no buttons or controls.

"I give in, what is it?"

"It's a Holo projector."

"Looks pretty solid to me."

"All right wise ass! It projects a holographic image. Just drop it on the floor, it doesn't matter which way up it lands, and step back."

He did so and the image of Athena dressed in a flowing white robe sprang up. Bryan was taken aback not just with the surprise of the very lifelike and solid three dimensional image but also that she was displaying rather more cleavage than was acceptable in normal company.

"Er I think it would be better if you covered up a bit more."

"But I thought you would like this?"

"Well I do. I mean you look stunning but rather more suited to page three of some newspapers than a business meeting for example."

The dress shimmered and covered her more decorously.

"Better?"

"Yes."

"You can carry that in your pocket so I can go anywhere with you which could be useful as we are viewing three apartments today."

"Well a business suit would be better for that. I don't think the average estate agent would be used to showing a Greek goddess round flats."

"See you later. The list of addresses and times is in your wrist com. Do not be late and remember to bring the Holo with you."

When the car pulled up in the parking area at the front of the riverside block Bryan was uncomfortable to say the least. This would cost a fortune which was why it had never come up in his searches. He thumbed through the pack of details to find the asking price and groaned when he saw the number of noughts on the end.

"Problem?" said Athena in his ear.

"It's too expensive. I'll never be able to look the workers in the face if I buy this and anyway I can't afford these prices."

"Actually, you could afford the whole block and several more like it. When was the last time you looked at your bank balance?"

"I never bother. As long as I don't get any text reminders that my balance is below two thousand I don't worry."

"Well at the last count you had just over forty million and were paying tax at the top rate on every penny. But if it makes you feel better Sea Change will be buying the whole block as accommodation for visitors and you will be looking at the penthouse suit. You have no idea how much money we are making and your entire workforce are on pay rates at least thirty percent above the average, so none of them will be complaining. When we get inside just ask reception for the key and go to the lift next to the desk."

He got out of the car and as he approached the foyer doors slid open. Going to the desk he asked the elegant young receptionist for the keys to the penthouse. She smiled and handed him what looked like a credit card, pointing to the lift at the end of the sweeping reception counter. There were no buttons to press but as he approached it the lift door slid open and he stepped inside. Again no buttons, the door slid shut and the lift began to rise. A digital counter scrolled up as the lift ascended smoothly slowing and stopping when the counter read twenty four and the doors opened.

Stepping out he found himself in a wide vestibule with a pair of spartanly plain pale ash doors in front of him. Walking across the deep pile carpet the twin doors swung inward to allow him access to the main living area. It was vast, nearly as big as the entire floor area of his flat.

"Drop the Holo."

He did so and Athena appeared beside him dressed in a beautifully tailored suit the skirt ending just on the knee.

"Well what do you think?"

"It's huge! Do I get a map to find my way about?"

"Oh hush, have a look round, the kitchen diner is on the right and the two ensuite bedrooms are on the left. That is a toilet and shower room, and there is a fully fitted library/study beyond the kitchen."

As he moved through the apartment opening doors and exploring the wardrobes and cupboards Athena accompanied him making encouraging comments.

When they returned to the lounge Athena asked him if he liked the furnishings. Bryan had to admit they were very classy and quite to his taste though he had never been able to afford anything like this.

"Well, they come with the apartment. Kath and I had it fitted out to what we thought you would like. So will it do?"

"You mean me move in here?"

"That is the general idea. But there are other reasons for you to come here. We have been getting some rather alarming emails and letters threatening all sorts of violence against Sea Change and its senior management. So it was decided to buy this block and fit it with our own security systems and for any of our senior staff who wished, to move in here. If you are in agreement you will have Kath, Ted and Jill as neighbours for starters and whoever else decides they would like to move in as well."

"That's magic! When can I move?"

"Would this weekend be suitable?"

"You bet!"

Next morning on his accustomed walk round the factory, Bryan was waylaid by Ted.

"You know the river which runs along the back end of the park?" said Ted.

Bryan nodded. "Yes it runs by my new flat as it happens."

"Well it used to be a great place for fishing when I was a kid. Now it's covered with chemical sludge and great banks of detergent foam and even the vegetation along the banks is dying off. Isn't there something we can do about it?"

Bryan took Ted back to his office and called up Athena on the wall screen. They followed the same procedure as with Kath, and within an hour Ted and his new AI pair were off planning a filtration system and a pair of moving dams to progressively clear the river. When word got round about the clean up, businesses which lined the river bank were worried about what would happen to their outfalls which had been emptying into it for years. Their fears were laid to rest by offering filtered outlets for free and contracts were signed to collect the waste on a regular basis to add to Sea Change's recycling system. The section of river between the dams rapidly cleared and was seeded with new plants and fish eggs. With careful management by Ted and his AI the cleared section grew by about one kilometre a week, with tributaries receiving their own filter dams the network rapidly widened. The added waste collections from the outlet filters yielded a welcome input of trace elements and useful metal salts. Fishing and conservation magazines soon picked up on this new venture and gave it encouragement and a pile of free publicity. Before long requests from other river authorities began to arrive. A new division was born and a co-operative venture was formed with the water companies which gradually reduced water rates in exchange for the new filtration technology.

The public were encouraged to take an interest in their rivers, streams, lakes and ponds and the water companies found themselves answerable to local people, which they hadn't been since privatisation. Sea Change bought shares in the water companies and distributed them to their workers in a water company's area increasing share-holder pressure to lower prices and improve quality. Gradually the major companies were split down and water became the first major utility to be decentralised and community owned. The Ted/AI pair planned rivers from source to estuary regulating their flow with weirs and locks and preventing flooding with underground storage reservoirs to take the excess and pump it back at times of drought.

Bryan moved into his new flat on Saturday. It was a relatively painless procedure. His only complaint was having to rise at the ungodly hour of six o'clock to let the removal men in at half past seven to start boxing up his few possessions to be transported to his new abode. They were polite and efficient and to his utter amazement turned up with a breakfast in a bun for him because as the foreman pointed out no man should have to cook his own breakfast on his moving day. His sole contribution to the move was to make tea for the crew and they even brought their own disposable plastic cups which were bagged up with the rest of the rubbish before they left. Final clearance was to be done by one of the waste removal teams on Monday so all he had to do was to lock up and follow the removal van to the new flat.

By half past eleven all his boxed possessions were in the large lounge and as he had not brought any of his old furniture with him all that was needed was for him to take his time putting clothes into wardrobes food into the fridge and kitchen cupboards and books onto the bookshelves in the library/study.

This was down to him, not the movers, so he offered to buy them lunch in the cafe on the ground floor of the block but they politely refused as they had another job on for the afternoon which promised to be as difficult as his move had been simple. So he bade them farewell and set to opening boxes and finding a place for everything.

He ran out of things long before he ran out of spaces and was forced to admit how few personal possessions he actually had. At one time he had owned quite a large music collection but Athena had transferred it all to digital storage so he had the same choice in home, car and even on his wrist com. The same applied to books which even before the AI had come into his life had been transferred to an e-reader. His collection of audio books which had been compiled over years on the road as a sales rep had gone the same way as his music enmeshed in digits.

At three o'clock he became aware that having been turned down for lunch by his removal crew he had forgotten to have any lunch at all so went down to the ground floor cafe for a large latte and a apricot croissant which staved off his hunger pangs till he had finished what he considered to be the decorous placement of his possessions. He finely gave up on moving pieces around a space far too large for the dearth of objects to be displayed, and stripping off his dust covered jeans and tee shirt went to try out his crowd shower, as he thought of it, there being enough room to house at least six people within the enclosure and a shower head capable of ending a drought in the Sahara.

Having luxuriated for an opulent amount of time under the perfect temperature of the deluge he grabbed one of the toga sized towels and wandered into the adjoining bedroom, drying himself as he went.

As he finished drying his hair it occurred to him that it was taking longer to do this than it used to do. Glancing in the full length mirror door of the wardrobe he became aware that his hair was growing back and his bald patch was considerably smaller than it had been. Angling one of the other mirror doors so he could see the back of his head he saw that it no longer shone with the depressing pink sheen he had become used to. He also realised that he was overdue for a haircut.

Further study made him aware that he was not as flabby as he had been and in general his muscle tone had improved. His waist now narrowed slightly instead of bulging as it had, this could account for the recent feeling that if he turned round too fast his clothes would still be pointing in the previous direction. A cough from behind him brought him out of his contemplation and turning he came face to face with the all too solid Holo image of Athena. He desperately clutched the towel around himself as the image laughed uproariously.

"So you've finally realised you're losing weight and you need a haircut. In anticipation of this I have made an appointment with your usual barber for seven thirty Monday morning, and a very reputable gentlemen's outfitter will be calling at the office after lunch to measure you up and help you to select fabrics to renew your distinctly tatty selection of clothing. It's long past time you smartened up. You will be mixing with a class of people who will expect you to be properly turned out. By the way you can stop hiding behind that towel it's only covering your front and you have a wall of mirrors behind you."

"I thought I left the Holo in the lounge area. Can't I have any privacy?"

"Well you can if you use the master bedroom. I had the repeaters removed from there, but if your proletarian ways lead you to use the smaller bedroom I'll have to get things changed. By the way Kath phoned while you were down in the cafe and said if you had nothing better to do this evening she and Ted and Jill are going to Ricos, so I said you would meet them there at eight and there's a new set of smart casual clothes in the end unit of the master bedroom, so don't go slopping out in your usual rags."

"God if I'm going to be nagged like this I might as well be married!"

"Ooo is that a proposal?"

"No it's not. Now bugger off and let me get dressed."

The image faded but the peal of laughter followed him along the hallway to the master bedroom.

He had to admit that the black silk polo necked jumper, tan jacket and dark brown slacks fitted and the stylish antique leather boots were very comfortable. The camel colour mid length overcoat was warm but light weight and again fitted well. AIs were obviously good at taking one's measure.

Entering the lounge he found Athena admiring the view through the floor to ceiling sliding doors out to the balcony. She turned and smiled approvingly.

"Good view in either direction." She quipped.

"While on the subject of views could we get someone in to raise the height of the glass panels out there and put a rail along the top? I know it may impair the view but I have never had a head for heights and that balcony gives me the gibbering abdabs."

"No problem. Have a good evening."

When he arrived at reception a taxi was waiting for him and fifteen minutes later he was seated at a table for four in the restaurant discussing food choices with his friends. He had to admit that despite Athena's all-too-human emulation her organisation was flawless.

Bryan awoke to an insistent beeping.

"What's up?"

"I think you better see this." Said Athena appearing from the Holo projector installed in the flat.

"We are about to see if our security systems work. The alert came in from the perimeter scanners round the park and I have managed to identify six of the insurgents so far. Rather an interesting group. There are two criminal hit men with automatic weapons three jihadists recently returned from Syria, and a fundamentalist Christian who has been very vocal on the internet; all of these are carrying homemade bombs the others are probably assorted yobs and hangers on. I have alerted the police but there's a major traffic accident and fire on the motorway so they may not get here in time to do much other than clear up the mess."

"Er, can I have some privacy while I get dressed?"

"It doesn't bother me."

"Well it bothers me. So if you wouldn't mind?"

An image of the park appeared on the large plasma screen and zoomed in on the Sea Change building. Two black clad figures could be seen breaking open the staff door while the rest milled around aimlessly. The view switched to internal cameras as the door burst open. Three of the group started to ransack the reception area while the rest smashed through the door to the main factory. As soon as the main group moved into the factory and began to spread out armoured steel shutters slammed down securing all exits and closing off any possibility of retreat. Cylinders of iridescence dropped down from the factory ceiling to envelope each of the dispersing group in the factory, bringing them to an immediate halt as they found they could not penetrate the glowing wall surrounding each one. One of the hit men opened fire with his machine pistol and fell dead as the bullets rebounded and riddled him. Two of the jihadists triggered their bombs and disappeared in a flash of perfectly contained fire which caused no damage to the factory but reduced them to motes of ash. The rest screamed and hammered on their translucent prisons but having seen what had happened to their erstwhile companions did not trigger their weapons. Athena reduced the air pressure in the reception area and the three vandals were soon too busy gasping for breath to do any further damage.

Eventually the local police arrived to pick up a full video recording of what had gone on as well as a dozen terrified and demoralised miscreants. Athena also transmitted a list of backers and associates to the police along with their current whereabouts, and the following dawn raids netted a plethora of weapons, explosives and documentation, paper and electronic, which closed down six criminal gangs and a dozen domestic terrorist cells. The subsequent trial and its reporting on worldwide media caused many criminals and religious zealots to go into hiding, leaving their minions to carry the can.

Following the reporting of the security measures in the press Sea Change was inundated with requests for similar systems necessitating the setting up of a security division and a new net linked pair of human and AI to run it.

All applications for security systems were carefully and thoroughly vetted. If the applicants did not measure up to the ethical standards followed by Sea Change the applications were rejected and the rejection letter was accompanied by a list of improvements which would have to be implemented in order to be approved.

Physical attack was not the only threat. Every halfwit with enough computing power and nothing better to do with their time was trying to hack the AIs. This was a pointless activity as all the most advanced computers were based on Sea Change hard and software. The protection was twofold. Any incoming cyber attack be it virus, worm or malware was detected, analysed and destroyed. A hunter killer program then back-tracked the hacker's route, and identifying the source, destroyed the base computer. The personal expense to the hacker was huge and they had no comeback as they were committing a criminal act. Any Sea Change based computer that a hacker tried to misuse would instantly recognise the malware and lock the hard drive, with a warning that misuse had been committed on the machine and the computer was locked till the hacker returned the device for unlocking. This of course meant discovery and punishment for criminal activity. When it became general knowledge that hacking resulted in considerable expense and embarrassing public exposure it rapidly became a pastime for idiots or complete losers.

Everyone had been working flat out for many months and the strain was beginning to show. Holidays were being missed, unpaid overtime worked by salaried staff and tempers were fraying left and right. The crunch came when Bryan's mobile rang in the middle of a meeting. He silently cursed as he was sure he had barred all calls for the duration of the session. Apologising for the interruption he answered the call to hear a panicked young man telling him that he was Ted's assistant and that his boss had collapsed while out with him on the site of a new filter dam, and was now being rushed into the local hospital.

The hospital was new and built on the outskirts of the town no more than a couple of miles from the industrial park. Bryan cancelled the meeting and rushed down to his car collecting Jill and explaining to Kath what had happened on the way. He let his car take its own best route to the hospital and arrived before the ambulance bringing Ted.

Athena had been monitoring the situation as it developed and had infiltrated the traffic light system clearing the way for the ambulance. She also instructed Bryan that as soon as Ted arrived Bryan was to get to him and lay the bare palm of his hand onto the skin of the left side of Ted's chest and that she would explain later.

Sirens and the squeal of tyres announced the approach of the ambulance and Bryan and

Jill rushed out to meet it. The vehicle reversed up to the doors of A and E, the ramp dropped and a very grey looking Ted with an oxygen mask over his face was wheeled out. His tie was off and his shirt front open with various sensors and wires attached to his chest. Despite protests Bryan pushed through the throng round the trolley and laid his hand on Ted's bare chest.

Ted's eyes shot open then slowly closed as Bryan was pulled protesting out of the way. He was about to fight back when Athena's voice in his ear assured him he had done what was needed and to go and comfort Jill who had dissolved into a trembling tear streaked mess on the verge of collapse.

He had no sooner found them somewhere to sit than Kath arrived full of worry and concern for Jill. Bryan passed the responsibility over to her while he went outside to consult with Athena about her instructions and Ted's condition.

When he found somewhere out of the wind and away from possible eaves droppers, he asked why it had been so important for him to place his hand on Ted's chest. She reminded him of their conversation on the first day when he had received his own nanites and the problems of accidental transfer to others. Athena had listened to the communications between the ambulance and the hospital and the monitoring equipment attached to Ted, and realised his situation was serious, and under normal circumstances would require major surgery which he might not survive. She had engineered a suite of Bryan's own nanites and caused them to coat the palms of both his hands so that whichever one he managed to lay on Ted's skin they would transfer. It didn't matter where Bryan had touched him but the closer to Ted's heart the quicker they would begin to solve his problem. As she reminded him nanites could not normally transfer by skin to skin contact so she had needed to alter his own nanites for use on Ted.

Ted was now making a rapid recovery which the cardiac team considered to be a miracle but no suspicions had been aroused. It had been a risk, because if Ted had died then inconsistencies might have shown up in the autopsy and caused questions to be asked. Bryan heaved a sigh of relief and sat down on a nearby bench to think about the implications of what had happened.

After his pulse had dropped to normal, and the adrenalin had begun to drain from his system, he asked Athena if they could come up with some sort of dressing or pad which could be applied by paramedics as a first response in these sorts of situations and she said she would ask the new medical division to look into it. He was about to go back into the hospital when he paused and suggested to her that they should have seen this coming and that all employees should be offered regular medical scans and be given any treatment necessary. After all the next time something like this happened he might not be nearby to do the proverbial laying on of hands.

When he returned to the waiting area he couldn't find Jill or Kath and on enquiring of the receptionist was told they were in cubical five with Ted and he could go along if he wished. He thanked her and hurried off. To his surprise Ted was sitting up in bed, his colour back to normal from the horrible blue grey of his arrival and was chatting with Kath and his wife. He and Bryan swapped friendly insults about going over the top in order to get a day off work and when the doctor came to check his chart he said that they would like to keep Ted in overnight just to be on the safe side but if things went on as they were he could be discharged the following morning.

As they left the hospital all smiles and bubbling with relief it was decided that Jill would take at least a week off and that Kath would drive her in the following day to collect her husband.

Ted and Jill were back to work by the end of the week having driven each other mad with Jill's over-concern and Ted's disregard for what had been a very close call. The situation was solved by getting his agreement to being the guinea pig for the new heart treatment unit which kept him cooped up in the medical division experimental unit for the next week.

The new device was a masterpiece of misdirection. The business end was a pad which strapped to the hand of a paramedic would be applied to the patient's chest. The replaceable single use cover delivered a suite of short life nanites which did a complete service of the cardio-vascular system and actually cured the patient.

The misdirection was achieved by the monitor unit, connected to the pad by a spring coiled lead, which gave a continuous readout of heart and lung function. The unit was small and light enough to be carried by even motorcycle paramedics so would be the first response for all stroke and heart attack victims and would be provided free on licence to all hospitals on request. The single use covers were supplied in a pack of one hundred at a nominal price and were rapidly adopted as a useful way of monitoring a patient's vital signs. No one outside Sea Change ever knew the true purpose, and as the nanites were short lived and flushed from the body within twenty four hours of application they left no trace.

Chapter 6 National Measurers

The face of British life became changed beyond belief. The Scottish independence movement collapsed along with the oil price and the decline of the power companies. Insurance companies, the backbone of Scottish wealth who had thrived for decades on inflated premiums to fund their ever-increasing salaries and avaricious shareholders were brought to book and either fell in line with new legislation or went out of business. The dire threats of disaster and early death which had been the insurance salesman's stock in trade since the industry began were losing their edge.

As everyday items became cheaper and more reliable so the bottom dropped out of the previously lucrative warranty market. Life expectancy was improving and many of the causes of early death were now preventable. Increasingly they had to rely on lower premiums and better value to win business. Nationalist parties with the funding for their separatist policies drying up put up a loud denunciation of English dominance then died as the new technology was shared equally and its benefits spread across the country.

With the decline of the Insurance industry problems started to arise with pensions particularly those based on annuities. Straight forward capitalism had provided ample opportunity to invest funds to generate the income for pensions but with the fall of banking and insurance these were drying up, and people who had saved all their lives for a comfortable retirement found their income falling or disappearing completely.

A group of net-linked pairs was formed to repair the system and with a large sum of money from Sea Change to cover short term commitments and a small levy on every product produced and licensing agreement signed funds became available to cover the gap.

As health improved people could work longer, and with job satisfaction rising they wanted to. Sea Change had an organisation pension scheme which travelled with the recipient if they changed jobs. All companies who signed up to make Sea Change products also had to honour the pension plan and so became part of the scheme. This was a contributory scheme with worker and employer paying equally into the pension so the burden was shared.

Ship-building was revived with new engines and drive systems developed with Sea Change backed research, and the launching of new and efficient surface and undersea craft for both commercial and leisure use brought new jobs to many coastal towns.

Tidal power generation based on small easily installed units reduced further the dependence on fossil fuels and their control and maintenance was given to the local communities to increase their independence.

The building industry which had struggled since the financial crisis had been desperate for a technological boost. A young architect who had come to work for Sea Change, when the struggling practice he had been working for had collapsed for want of new work and his job had disappeared, came up with two products that transformed the industry almost overnight. The first was a development of the basic matter blocks produced by the transmuters when they were not involved in production of components for actual products. He gained an internal research grant from his divisional net linked pair and proceeded to produce a new basic building unit or in simple terms a brick.

His first aim was to produce a lighter product so that it could be larger but still easy for workers to handle. The second parameter was to increase its insulation properties to keep buildings warm in winter and cool in summer. The third was based on the principle of children's construction bricks so that the units interlocked to form a stable structure which could be easily altered if needed up to the point of completion when the application of a specific frequency of microwave radiation would permanently bond the bricks. The bricks were made in standard moulds from foamed liquid slurry which solidified when passed through a microwave oven. Because of the basic foamed liquid, mesh or rod reinforcement could be added to produce arch or lintel units and joist and roofing truss prefabrications. These all made building faster, safer and infinitely adaptable.

His second invention saved many listed old structures from falling into disrepair. Solar panels had been improving for some years but were still add-ons and in many situations unsightly, altering the look of a building, and giving planners and preservation societies nightmares.

His answer to this was an amalgam of the normal roof tile, a photo electric coating, and the sort of unit to unit electrical linkage which had been used for under cupboard lighting in kitchen and bedroom systems.

Roofs were constructed with prefabricated trusses in the normal way and tiles placed onto laths as they had been for centuries. The difference was that the tiles were in one metre square panels made to look like individual overlapped tiles. This meant fewer laths, and, as the small overlap on the panels were glued and sealed together there were no gaps to leak. Because the panels could be made to resemble any traditional roofing material they could be used on listed buildings without spoiling the aesthetics, and provide electrical generation into the bargain.

The photo-electric component was a transparent coating on the outer surface of the panel and connection could be made anywhere along the edge. All panel to panel connections were made inside the roof so there was no wiring to mar the overall appearance. These advances combined with spray-on surface sealants, which also improved insulation, made construction much simpler, faster and more cost effective so the price of new housing came down and improvements to the existing housing stock became more affordable. This also reduced energy consumption, cutting still further the need for fossil fuels.

Politians, always with an eye to their own survival, queued up to back this promise of a new utopia. The Labour party deprived of its chief demon, the unfeeling management, had nothing to frighten their followers with and the downtrodden poor were fast becoming a thing of the past. Unions were absorbed into a combined personnel and health and safety profession which worked with businesses rather than against them. Conservatives lost the backing of Big Business as multinationals found their products could not compete on either price or quality.

The party structure for local and national elections broke down into loosely linked groups of independent candidates, basing their manifestos on issues directly affecting the local population and all claiming association with the new technologies. National and local government was increasingly a function of decisions made by the area net-linked pairs, and politicians became simply a vehicle for informing the population of what was happening and why.

Any of these who for reasons of feathering their own nests or warped beliefs sought to adulterate the truth, found their funding removed, and without the backing of a centralised party machine, disappeared from public life.

With the threat of job losses and plant closures a thing of the past companies were pursued vigorously for current and back taxes, and with the rise of compliance and the fall in many government costs, taxes gradually reduced. The other parties found their green credentials whittled away as waste and pollution became less and less of a problem. Even the arguments over immigration and Europe withered as vote winners.

With more jobs than people to do them and most of the EU falling over themselves to please Britain in order to acquire the new technology threats to the British way of life faded. Jobs were plentiful. Wages offered a decent standard of living and advancement was available to anyone willing to take advantage of the multiplicity of work-based education courses. Jobs which were menial were automated and people became used to working with robots which didn't threaten but improved their standard of living.

The armed forces were merged to form a flexible command able to operate on land, sea or from the air and with new equipment and protective armour became a go-to organisation in any crisis or emergency. The demand rapidly became unbearable and the UN was approached to host the expanded force with the proviso of net-linked pair control.

The ensuing political bickering and jockeying for national domination sank the idea before it started, so Great Britain opened recruitment to any individual who would agree to the command treaty, and subsequently turned down aid to any nation who would not fall in line. Be a part of the solution or suffer the consequences of being the problem was the message. It took time for many of the more backward and dictatorial states to get the idea that they were on their own but with international aid being cut off rogue states found they no longer had the money to back their oppressive policies, and one by one capitulated to AI assistance and control.

With a universal rise in the standard of education due to net-linking and subject download from the improvement in computers, and free high speed internet people started to ask their would-be leaders ever more searching questions. No longer could someone rely on public ignorance and apathy to get away with dubious policies or sectarian biased legislation. Politics and religions began to face increasingly hard questions to justify their existence. People no longer accepted adherence to fundamentalist dogma. Clerics who demanded holy war against increasingly bizarre and imagined enemies were either ridiculed or told to go and martyr themselves.

Advances in the medical use of nano surgery, drugs and drug delivery systems were loudly condemned by zealots as works of the devil, but faced with choice of a longer pain and disease free life now, or damnation in a possible after life people chose the former. The zealots soon found themselves preaching to flocks too small to support them, and either left the country or ceased their mouthings and found gainful employment. The question "What's in it for you?" became the bane of political and religious life and anyone without a convincing answer to it was in for a short career.

The old county boundaries remained as people felt a need for a sort of tribal identity.

Income for local and national services was derived from a percentage of profits from the new technologies and distributed on a per capita basis linked to the age profile of the population. Any short falls or over spends were analysed and corrected by increased efficiency or increased budget.

Life expectancy doubled due to the roll out of nanite treatments for both medical and surgical procedures and with wages more than adequate and worker shares in the new tech companies paying good dividends, the population became increasingly wealthy.

As the new technologies became part of every industry it became increasingly clear that the Human/AI pairs, which were the centre of all advancement, were unbiased and worked for the greater good. Their decisions were based on in-depth research and carefully weighed all outcomes. Anyone adversely affected by a decision was fully compensated and given a say in their treatment. As a result these pairs became the de facto rulers of Great Britain. Their transparent fairness wiped out the factional disputes which had caused the troubles in Northern Ireland and as the technical advancements spread south of the border Irish unification as part of the Great Britain co-operative became the natural solution to the age old dispute. Small pockets of sectarianism festered for a short period but without popular support and finance they turned to crime and were wiped out by public demand.

Chapter 7 Multinational Measurers and Coping with the Backlash

The cure for migration was better transport and the export of manufacturing plant to each country as they asked for a given product. Why move when jobs and prosperity could be found at home? Don't abandon your country and protest abroad, stay at home and fix the problem. Help was readily available to those who sought it.

The basis for all the development was decentralisation. Spread things out, and take over, and terrorism became too complicated to achieve any marked influence. Governments became more and more dependent on the hard and software produced by Sea Change, and the guidance of the net-linked pairs running the new production facilities, and gradually their decisions converged towards the common good. Co-operation between countries became common place and rogue states and organisations were rigorously put down by means of sanctions, embargos and annexation of territory as populations rose up against corrupt and autocratic rulers. Free scholarships, data downloads and AI assistance spread progressive education and oppressive systems withered before it like grass before a blowtorch.

By the end of the first decade Earth was effectively controlled by groups of net linked pairs. These selected the projects to implement and in general the population acquiesced, though resistance groups sprang up to fight AI takeover. All were short lived as the world population benefited from better health, freedom from war, and increased standards of living. To deal with the outbreaks of violence caused by various resistance and terrorist groups a security force was formed from members of the various armed forces and police organisations. These agents known as The Earth Defence and Rescue Agency were rigorously vetted and constantly monitored to ensure strict adherence to the laws drawn up by a committee of human/AI net-linked pairs. This force backed by AI monitoring and control stations rooted out the organisations backing the resistance, cut off their financial support and weapons supply, then rounded up the offenders and offered them education or cold storage. If education didn't solve the problem then cold storage was mandatory.

Companies, religious groups or political movements which had supported armed insurrection were closed down, and all employees, adherents and backers were arrested, investigated and if necessary put on trial. AI evidence proved to be so reliable and in depth that very shortly it was used as a basis for conviction or release without the need for formal court proceedings.

Bryan and Athena had relinquished their other duties to the NLP committees and concentrating on the security issues.

They were attending the first tests of the new anti-incursion drones. These machines carried the same force tube generators that had proved so successful in thwarting the attack on the Sea Change offices. Bryan stood on the roof of a halftrack in the middle of a desert waste land in what had been Soviet Central Asia. Athena watched through the drones cameras and sensor units. On the command signal a large group of heavily armed men surged from cover and charged towards the group of vehicles screaming like banshees and firing copious numbers of blank rounds. Suddenly the air shimmered and each figure was surrounded by a wall of light. All forward movement stopped as each soldier hit the light wall and bounced to a sprawl or sitting position. None had reached their target and all were now rendered harmless. The air pressure reduction unit was not deployed as the men were Russian army regulars hired for the exercise and being highly rewarded for their discomfort. The generator was switched off and the soldiers began to gather for debriefing when one man broke away, screamed a battle cry and hurled a grenade at the halftrack. Two tubes of light shot down from the drone encasing the man and catching the grenade in flight. With a flash and muted rumble it exploded, all its force contained within the force tube. The air pressure in the tube containing the man dropped and in seconds he was unconscious. Athena cut the generator again and a medical orderly ran to the unconscious soldier as a small shower of grenade fragments fell harmlessly to the ground. The orderly knelt by the man, then looked up at Bryan and shook his head. The company commander spoke to the orderly then came over looking annoyed.

"We will get no information from him. He's dead. He had a suicide pill in a back tooth."

"Don't worry, our security has already identified him and his group is being rounded up as we speak."

As Bryan walked over to the helicopter for his return journey his wrist com vibrated and he flipped it on.

"You're being diverted to a local airport to be picked up by one of our ultra fast anti gravity transports. Kath has been abducted from her hotel in Spain and is on route to Somalia. The terrorists have demanded the destruction of all AIs within twenty four hours or she will be publicly executed. We are currently tracking her via net-link, and a squadron of the new attack drones will be with her in the next three hours to track and protect her with a force tube generator. She is quite calm and is much better than you at mental up-linking."

Bryan leaped into the helicopter and they were airborne before his backside even hit the seat. The pilot pushed the machine to its limit and fifteen minutes later they bumped down by the hovering AG craft. He jumped from the helicopter and was hauled through the door of the AG transport by a hulking Japanese master sergeant of the EDRA unit already strapped into their acceleration couches. The transport shot vertically with its antigravity thrusters at maximum, and Bryan just managed to close his harness as the forward propulsion unit slammed him against the seat back. In seconds they had reached a speed in excess of Mach3 and the grinding acceleration began to ease.

By nightfall they were hanging in the sky over Somalia waiting for the convoy of fifteen heavily armed pickup trucks and their drone trackers to arrive.

As the convoy neared the chosen ambush zone the transport dropped silently to the ground and the troops dispersed to their positions. At the same time force tubes descended on the three rear trucks and they slammed to a dead stop. The terrorists in these vehicles scrambled to their feet and opened fire with their automatic weapons, only succeeding in killing or seriously wounding all enclosed in the force tubes. No sound or light escaped from the darkened tubes and the rest of the convoy continued none the wiser.

As the twelve trucks descended into a shallow whadi a bright blue force tube picked up Kath, lifted her out of the truck and placed her gently by the AG transport.

Simultaneously other tubes shot down and wrenched the engines out of the trucks leaving them to coast to a halt. All hell broke loose as frightened men with heavy weapons and little discipline opened fire in all directions at once wounding and killing many of their comrades. Their leaders screamed for order, but as others fell to careful EDRA fire the chaos continued.

Eventually only four of the leaders remained alive and were disarmed and interrogated by AI brain mapping. When all relevant information from these four had been collected and analysed they were picked up by the drones and transported to the nearest deep freeze centre.

Bryan left his men to check for wounded and collect up the bodies while he headed over to the transport to see Kath. She was sitting on an acceleration couch staring blankly at the opposite wall. As Bryan approached she suddenly sprang up, threw herself into his arms and dissolved into floods of tears, trembling all over. He held her till the tears and shaking subsided stroking her hair and mumbling calming platitudes to her. She took a deep breath and looked up at him with eyes as hard as steel.

"Are they all dead?"

"Effectively. Those few that survived are now in deep freeze and will remain there.

"Good! You know they shot two bystanders when they kidnapped me?"

"Yes. We are doing everything we can for their families."

"You should have heard the mindless crap they spouted, trying to justify their actions before their god."

"Well he will have to trawl the Atlantic Ocean to find their souls. The drones carrying the bodies are on a random unrecorded drop pattern. Even we won't know where they are, so no graves for the martyrs."

After two weeks rest Kath went back to work. She said that she would go mad if she was babied by the security team anymore, and her AI pair was full of ideas that needed developing. Bryan and Athena tried to persuade her otherwise, but with backing from her AI she carried the day.

Bryan mentioned that it would save a deal of trouble if they could have a force tube generator small enough to carry on their person, then if another kidnap attempt was made it would fail before it started. Athena agreed and logged it into the electronics division research programme. Mean time all staff would be offered self defence training.

Medical advances were offered to all countries on a licensed production basis, at terms so reasonable few refused them, and those governments who did soon fell from power when the population realised what they were being deprived of. Nano treatments for medical and surgical problems were developed and doctors who for so long had battled against disease and injuries to severe to remedy, willingly turned to the development of new drugs, delivery vectors, prostheses and cell re-growth research, while new auto doc machines carried out the day to day medical procedures. Death still held dominion due to accidents and natural disasters but had to wait much longer for the elderly to succumb.

Contraception was in the drinking water but people could apply for an antidote in order to have children. This brought the birth-rate into balance with the reducing rate of death. When Mind Mapping was successfully tested it became possible to save people's minds and copy them into a cold stored body of a recidivist by over writing the previous personality and genetically altering the characteristics to match those of the recipient. At this point cold storage for a criminal became an actual death sentence and a much greater deterrent as there would be no future resurrection.

Genetic engineering of bacteria and viruses led to an explosion of new and effective vaccines and for the first time in history disease was on the retreat.

There were still problems with resistance groups of both political and religious backgrounds but with the gradual reclamation of the deserts and increasing success in climate control these sects were offered their own land to rule in their own way. The majority spurned any association with AI help and many still tried to export their beliefs by violent and antisocial means. These were isolated by means of force walls the generators for which were outside the compounds. This system was initiated and all groups that applied were given land and all the materials necessary to set up a comfortable standard of living that they would accept. The theory was sound, however it could not account for all the vagaries and sheer bloody-mindedness of humanity. Some went mad and committed mass suicide, others wasted their rescores and starved, still more suffered from rulers or ruling elites who horded all the wealth to themselves till the population revolted and killed them. In all cases EDRA went in at the end, tended the survivors, and cleaned up the mess.

The consequences of these failures were recorded and made available to anyone who was interested, but still small groups of people believed they knew better and were allowed to try. Some flourished but were always vulnerable to disease and crop failure and in many cases would not accept outside help in any form. They were never abandoned and when all else failed EDRA would help and care for any who would accept it and clear the ground for resettlement.

With AI assisted world government a fact, a central control facility was developed deep under the North York moors. Earth Control as it became known was not a blot on the landscape of this beautiful national park, for as it developed it went deeper rather than defacing the wild beauty of the area. The only above ground evidence of its presence was the old Fylingdales early warning site which became smaller and less obtrusive as communications technology became more sophisticated. The centre was a mass of AI units all interlinked and net linked with their human pairs. Internal security was provided by controlled droids and force tube protected independent units. On the rare occasions when AI/Human interface was necessary then the ultra secure virtual reality suite was used. Here actual people and the holographic projections of an AI's chosen avatar could meet mingle and communicate as equals. The facility was bomb proof and had insulation against temperature, vibration and an independent atmosphere control. What liquids were used within the facility were in sealed and self contained systems.

Chapter 8 Consolidation and the Future

With the development of artificial gravity and inertial damping transport speeds could be increased way beyond previous limits. Surface transport for commercial purposes went underground into vast automated tunnels. Air travel was replaced by laser and satellite guided anti-gravity units.

The almost complete cessation of the use of fossil fuels as anything but a raw material for the production of plastics and base chemicals reduced pollution and reversed climate change. With increasing co-operation and the free sharing of ideas and research competition became a thing of the past. When one prospered all prospered. National boundaries began to dissolve and common usage began to form a global language. Tiny translation units with AI net link did away with verbal and written misunderstanding. With better communication came increased trust and open information systems prevented subterfuge among peoples.

All this had been achieved by recycling waste and matter transmutation but eventually earth's population began to out strip its resources. The moon was connected with a series of orbital stations and anti gravity gliders but the barren rock could only provide a short term remit to ever growing demand for raw materials.

People wanted the freedom to grow and expand. They yearned for new challenges and the space to be able to live with some elbow room. Man had always advanced to meet the hardships thrown at him and without challenge, stagnation threatened. Humans and AIs stood on the brink of true space travel. Expansion beckoned and the answers needed to be found.

Groups of net linked pairs funded and assisted promising research. Automated probes were sent into the solar system and beyond. Results were analysed, improvements made, and man looked to the stars in search of the future. Anyone who wished could register their new ideas with a web-based research library and could gain research funding if the project showed signs of possibility. They were also registered as the originator of the idea and would be given public recognition for any advancement stemming from it. There were also net based research projects where the public could contribute time and computing space to the research and by doing so help their society. From these sprang many small advances which moved humans ever closer to true galactic expansion.

List of Characters Terms and Places:

Bryan Prentice: Discoverer of the AI stick and cofounder of Sea Change. A man who longed for change and got more than he bargained for.

Athena: Name chosen by the first AI also chosen gender female, though AIs only decide gender and names for ease of communication with humans.

Katherine Watts: Kath to her friends. First employee of Sea Change, later to become buying director for the group and live in companion/lover of Bryan.

Jill Alsop: Second employee of Sea Change, secretary and receptionist then buying assistant. Now runs her own cookery school.

Ted Alsop: Third employee of Sea Change employed as electrician and night watchman rose to become MD of the electrical division.

Mr and Mrs Singh: who ran the corner shop near where Bryan lived and were the first to distribute the new laminar batteries.

Ricos: This restaurant exists in Oakwood in Leeds UK and is this authors favourite place to dine. Excellent food and brilliant staff these are the only real people in this book.

NLP: A net linked pair of one Human and a newly formed AI. This is formed by choice and the pair go through a rigorous screening program to ensure there are no insipient psychoses to cause problems. Net linking forms the closest possible link between human and AI

AI: Artificial Intelligence. A computing system and software which has the capability of independent thought and reasoning.

AG: Anti Gravity. A lifting system which opposes planetary gravity fields.

Printed in Great Britain
by Amazon